Will Stephanie Be
the Clip-on Queen Forever . . . ?

"Want to see my new earrings?" Stephanie asked as she took her jewelry box from her dresser. "They're really funky."

But expressions of horror and disgust came over the faces of the two Jennifers as they looked at the earrings.

"These are clip-ons!" Jennifer S. cried. "They all are!"

Stephanie snapped the lid shut. "Well, I wear clip-ons that look like pierced earrings," she explained.

"Clip-ons are so . . . second grade," Jennifer P. added.

Stephanie had to think quickly. "I know they are," she said. "That's why I'm definitely getting my ears pierced at the mall this weekend."

"Really?" the Jennifers said together. They were impressed.

Now Stephanie only had one tiny problem. Her dad had said she was still too young to get her ears pierced! What was she going to do?

FULL HOUSE

THAT'S THE WAY
IT CRUMBLES, COOKIE

FULL HOUSE

THAT'S THE WAY IT CRUMBLES, COOKIE

by Suzanne Weyn

Based on the series FULL HOUSE™ created by
Jeff Franklin

and on episodes written by
Tom Amundsen
Sarit Catz & Gloria Ketterer

A PARACHUTE PRESS BOOK

Parachute Press, Inc.
156 Fifth Avenue
New York, New York 10010

Special thanks to Michelle Sucillon, Lynne Fox, Karen McTier,
Amy Weingartner, Grace Ressler, and Karen Miller.

ISBN: 0-938753-77-0
Printed in the United States of America
September 1993
10 9 8 7 6 5 4 3 2 1

For Matthew Loomis,
a great friend

ONE

Michelle Tanner burst through her front door. "What a day!" she cried unhappily. She tossed her backpack onto the living room couch and slumped into a chair.

Danny Tanner, who was Michelle's dad, her uncle Jesse, and Danny's friend Joey were in the living room. "Fried baloney in the lunchroom again?" Uncle Jesse joked.

Michelle folded her arms and looked at Uncle Jesse crossly. She wasn't in a laughing mood. "I wish," Michelle said in a sulky voice. "The problem is much worse than that!"

Her tall, dark-haired father came over. "Tell you what," said Danny, putting his hand on her shoulder. "Let's head down to Johnson's Hardware, and you can tell Dad all your problems while you ride Quacky the mechanical duck."

Michelle rolled her eyes. "Quacky?" she asked. "Dad, I'm in second grade. I'd look silly on a mechanical duck."

Just then, Michelle's 11-year-old sister Stephanie came in the front door. "So, did Michelle tell you her bad news?" she asked everyone in the room.

"She's too old to ride Quacky?" Danny guessed.

"No, Dad. She's bummed because they're going to cancel the second-grade play. It's bad news for me, too. I was going to be the choreographer."

"What's that mean?" Michelle asked Stephanie.

"I was going to make up steps for the dances and teach them to the kids," Stephanie explained. "Plus, I was going to get extra credit for it. But now the show has been canceled. My first job as a choreographer, and I've already been fired."

"What a shame," said Danny.

Stephanie agreed. She'd had such great ideas for the play. "The mother who was going to direct it had to drop out. The company she works for is transferring her to another town," Stephanie continued. "Our only hope is to find a parent volunteer to direct the play." Stephanie stared meaningfully at Joey and Uncle Jesse. They weren't parents, but they were adults who lived with the Tanners in the same house. Jesse was their uncle. Joey wasn't actually a relative, but he was just like an uncle to them.

Michelle and Stephanie had an older sister, D.J., who was 17. When the girls' mother died, years ago, the house felt very empty. So their dad invited Uncle Jesse to move in. Then, when Joey Gladstone had needed a place to stay, Danny invited him to come live with the Tanners. After a while, Uncle Jesse married Becky. Then their twin boys were born, and all of them continued living in the house. And then there was Steve, D.J.'s boyfriend, and her best friend, Kimmy Gibbler, who were always hanging out at the house. That was okay by Michelle and Stephanie. They loved having a full house.

Joey and Uncle Jesse had always helped take care of the kids. They did a lot of the things regular parents did. So, Stephanie figured, why couldn't they direct the play?

Jesse and Joey knew very well what Stephanie was hinting at. But neither volunteered. Instead, they slumped lower into the living room couch.

"Don't you guys worry," Danny told Stephanie and Michelle. "I'm a parent. I volunteer."

Uncle Jesse and Joey looked relieved. "Danny, you beat us to it," Joey joked.

"You are so lucky," Uncle Jesse added with a sly smile. "I only wish it was me and Joey working with a stageful of those lovable little tykes."

"Thanks, Dad, but rehearsals are every morning at ten. That's when you do your

4

show," said Stephanie. Her dad and Aunt Becky were the hosts of *Wake Up, San Francisco*, a TV show that was on every morning. Danny would be busy during the only time the class could get the school auditorium.

Danny frowned and said, "I'm sorry, girls."

Once again, Michelle and Stephanie stared at Joey and Uncle Jesse. "Oh, boys," Michelle sang out in a super-sweet, coaxing voice.

This time, Joey and Uncle Jesse sank even lower into the couch. They looked as if they were trying to disappear altogether. "I guess your wish is going to come true," said Michelle. "You're going to get to work with all us lovable little tykes."

"Oh, goody," said Uncle Jesse, looking sick.

But Joey sat forward and smiled. "Ah, come on, Jesse," he said. "It'll be fun."

"Hurray!" Michelle cried.

"O-kay! All right!" Stephanie cheered as she and her sister ran to Uncle Jesse and Joey. The girls planted kisses on their cheeks and wrapped them in hugs.

"What's the play?" Joey asked.

"*America the Beautiful*," Michelle told him.

"It's about America."

As she spoke, Becky came into the living room from the kitchen. Becky was very beautiful, with long brown hair.

Toddling in behind Becky were the twins, Alex and Nicky.

"Jesse," Becky said, "do you have time to watch Nicky and Alex while I run to the store? They're getting so big that by the time I get them both in the cart, there's no room for any groceries."

"Sorry, Beck," Jesse said as he and Joey got up from the couch. "We've got to get down to the station." Uncle Jesse and Joey had their own radio show. They played CDs and even acted out the commercials. Uncle Jesse was a musician, and Joey wanted to be a comedian. Joey could imitate lots of funny characters such as Popeye and Bullwinkle the Moose. He used these characters' voices when he acted out the commercials with Jesse.

"Beck, I'd be happy to watch the boys for you," said Danny.

"Thanks, Danny," Becky replied happily as she hurried out the door with Jesse and Joey.

Danny took the twins by the hand and led them toward the door. "Nicky, Alex, you want to ride a mechanical duck?"

"Quack, quack, quack!" Nicky and Alex shouted in delight.

"I guess that means yes," Stephanie said to Michelle.

"All right. We sure are going to have fun now," Danny said to the twins. "You guys got any quarters?"

"Oh, Dad," said Michelle. Of course the twins didn't have quarters. Like Jesse and Joey, Danny was always joking around.

As Danny and the twins left, D.J. came walking in from the kitchen with her cute boyfriend, Steve.

"Guess what!" Michelle cried excitedly. "I'm going to be in *America the Beautiful*. Will you come see it?"

D.J. smiled. "We'd love to."

"We would?" Steve asked.

"Of course we would," D.J. insisted. "It's the cutest, sweetest, most adorable little play. You know, I was Yankee Doodle in that play when I was in the second grade."

"So was I," Stephanie added.

"Both of you?" Michelle asked, impressed. She looked at her sisters with admiration.

Stephanie was so sweet and smart. Michelle loved her yellow blond hair and upturned nose. Stephanie was good at sports and had lots of friends.

Michelle thought D.J. was also the greatest. At 17, she seemed almost a grown-up. And she was so pretty. Her dark blond hair was very long, and she wore it lots of different ways. Michelle could never decide if she wanted to be just like D.J. or just like Stephanie, so she'd decided to be just like both of them.

But Michelle wondered if she'd ever be as pretty and wonderful as her sisters. She hoped so. And a good place to start would be by keeping up the Tanner tradition of playing Yankee Doodle in the second-grade play. "I've got to be Yankee Doodle too," she said firmly.

"Okay," said Stephanie. "But you're going to have to work for it. Are you ready for that, Michelle?"

Michelle wasn't exactly sure what she

meant. "I guess so," she said in a small voice.

"I can't hear you," Stephanie pressed.

"I guess so!" Michelle shouted.

"Good!" said Stephanie. She threw back her shoulders as if she were a drill sergeant in the army. "We have a lot of work to do if you're going to get this part. You have to beat out a lot of other kids. But if you're serious, I'll help you."

Stephanie had no doubt that Michelle could win the part. She was adorable, with her wispy, reddish blond hair and big eyes. She wasn't shy, and she was loaded with talent. Still, it wouldn't be fair for Joey and Uncle Jesse just to hand her the part.

"I'm ready to begin work," said Michelle.

"Okay, then," said Stephanie. "Let's start practicing right now. March into the living room. Move!"

Playing along, Michelle began marching.

Stephanie looked over her shoulder at Steve and D.J. "I think I'm going to like this job," she said with a giggle.

TWO

"Okay, Michelle, let's try the song again," Stephanie said an hour later. She and Michelle were still in the living room, preparing Michelle for her big Yankee Doodle song-and-dance audition.

"I have a question," said Michelle, looking puzzled. "You know the part where Yankee Doodle sticks the feather in his hat and calls it macaroni?"

"Yeah, what about it?" Stephanie asked.

"Is he calling the feather macaroni or the hat macaroni?"

"The feather," Stephanie answered.

"Then what does he call the hat?" Michelle asked.

Stephanie had no idea. But at that moment, the doorbell rang. *Saved by the bell*, she thought.

Danny Tanner had come back with the twins a few minutes ago. They'd both fallen asleep in the car, and he'd carried them right upstairs to bed. Now he came down the stairs and answered the door.

When the door opened, Stephanie's eyes went wide with surprise. Standing on her front porch were two of the prettiest, most popular girls in the sixth grade, Jennifer S. and Jennifer P. Everyone added the initial of their last names so that they wouldn't get the two Jennifers confused.

The Jennifers and all the other popular sixth graders sat at the same table in the cafeteria. Lately, the Jennifers had started paying attention to Stephanie. So far they hadn't invited her to sit with them at lunch, but Stephanie was hoping they would soon. To sit at their table meant you were the coolest of the cool.

Their visit was a very good sign. They had never been to Stephanie's house before.

"Hi, is Stephanie here?" asked Jennifer S. "I'm Jennifer."

"And I'm Jennifer too," Jennifer P. added. Then she giggled. "Not number two, but also."

"Hi, Jennifer, Jennifer," Danny said. "Stephanie is right here with Michelle."

Michelle! Stephanie started to panic. She couldn't let the Jennifers know she was playing with her little sister. How uncool! "No, Michelle," she said loudly. "I can't play with you today. You know I never play with you!"

Michelle looked at Stephanie with a confused expression, wondering if her older sister had gone crazy.

"Jennifer! Jennifer!" Stephanie said as she hurried to the door. "What are you doing here?"

"We thought we'd stop by," said Jennifer S. As she spoke, her eyes wandered around the living room. Stephanie got the feeling she was judging the house. Maybe this was some final, ultimate check before they invited her to the cafeteria table.

"Great! Welcome," said Stephanie. "Come on in." She stepped back to let the Jennifers inside.

"I'll be upstairs with the twins if you need me," Danny said.

"Oh, we won't need you," Stephanie said as he went back upstairs. She didn't want the Jennifers to think she was a baby who always called on her dad for help.

"Hey, what about me?" Michelle cried, standing beside her sister. "I thought we were going to go over the song again."

"Oh, dear," Stephanie said, turning to the Jennifers. "She's acting so weird. She must be running a fever." Stephanie put her hand on Michelle's forehead. "She's absolutely burning up. I'll be right back. I have to pack her in ice, or she'll burn up."

"Shouldn't you tell your dad?" Jennifer P. asked.

"No, no," said Stephanie. "He relies on me to handle all family health emergencies."

Putting her arm around Michelle, Stephanie hurried her into the kitchen. "I don't feel sick," Michelle said the minute they were through the door.

"Of course you're not sick. I just don't want the Jennifers to know I was hanging out with you," Stephanie explained honestly. "No offense, but you *are* only in the second grade. I want the Jennifers to think I'm cool so they'll invite me to sit with them in the cafeteria."

"Big wow," said Michelle.

"Look, these are the coolest kids in the sixth grade," said Stephanie. "Just leave us alone."

"They don't look so cool to me," Michelle insisted.

"Well, they are," said Stephanie. "Michelle, I'm begging you. Stay out of our room for the next hour. Okay?"

Michelle made a face at her sister. "It isn't fair. It's my room too," she reminded Stephanie.

"Stay out of the bedroom and I promise the next time I do something really, really important in our room, you can be there. Deal?"

Michelle thought about this a moment. She

was a little tired of singing "Yankee Doodle" anyway. Sticking out her hand to shake, she said, "Deal."

Stephanie shook Michelle's hand and said, "D.J. and Steve are out in the yard. You can go bother them."

Through the back kitchen window, Michelle saw D.J. and her boyfriend at the picnic table in the yard. "Good idea," she said.

As Michelle went outside, Stephanie went back to the living room. "Excuse the interruption," she told the Jennifers. "She's got an ice pack on her forehead. I'm sure she'll be fine. Now, let's go up to my room."

She led them upstairs to the bedroom she shared with Michelle on the second floor. Suddenly the room looked very babyish to Stephanie. She didn't know why she'd never noticed it before.

Stephanie decided she had to find something to impress the Jennifers. Spying her new sunglasses on top of her dresser, she thought, *They're pretty cool.* She snapped them up and put them on. "What do you think of my new sunglasses?" she asked.

"Those are totally out of style," said Jennifer S.

In a flash, Stephanie snatched off the glasses and threw them on the floor. "That's why I don't wear them anymore."

"Did you see *Arsenio* last night?" Jennifer P. asked.

The Arsenio Hall Show was on way past Stephanie's bedtime. But she couldn't let the Jennifers know that. What could be more uncool than having a bedtime? "I was asleep," she said.

The Jennifers exchanged quick looks.

"I mean I fell asleep from barking so much," Stephanie added, knowing that the audience on *The Arsenio Hall Show* liked to bark and wave their arms in a circle when Arsenio appeared. Thank goodness she'd seen the tape Uncle Jesse had made of the show the night his favorite rock band was on.

Just to prove she knew what she was talking about, Stephanie began barking and waving her arm in a circle. The Jennifers joined in. *Good*, thought Stephanie. *They believe me.*

When they were done barking, Jennifer S. sat on Stephanie's bed. "Actually, I wasn't really watching the show last night either. I was shaving my legs."

"Me too!" Jennifer P. cried as if this was a wonderful coincidence.

At once, the two girls looked down at Stephanie's legs. Stephanie wished she were wearing jeans, but she was wearing a jean skirt. There was no getting out of this one. There was definitely a covering of fine blond hair on her long legs. "I was going to shave my legs," she bluffed. "But . . . uh . . . I like a little stubble. It keeps my socks up."

Again, a doubtful glance passed between the Jennifers.

Stephanie was panicking. This was going badly. She had to do something to prove she was cool. Then she remembered her new dangly paper-mâché banana earrings. They were absolutely the coolest. "Want to see my new earrings?" she asked as she took her jewelry box from her dresser. "They're really funky."

Stephanie opened the box and presented the earrings proudly. These would wow them.

But expressions of horror and disgust came

over the faces of the Jennifers as they looked at the earrings. *What?* Stephanie wondered. *What was wrong?*

"These are clip-ons!" Jennifer S. cried. She looked at Stephanie's open jewelry box. "They *all* are!"

Stephanie threw the earrings into the box and snapped the lid shut.

"We always thought you had pierced ears," said Jennifer P. Her tone of voice told Stephanie that pierced ears were extremely important.

"Well, I wear clip-ons that look like pierced earrings," Stephanie explained, hoping this would be good enough.

The Jennifers shook their heads. "No way," they said together.

"Clip-ons are so . . . second grade," Jennifer P. added.

Stephanie had to think of something quickly. She could sense that her seat at the cafeteria table was being pulled out from under her. "I know they are," she said. "That's why I'm definitely getting my ears pierced at the mall this weekend."

The Jennifers smiled brightly. "Really? We'll be at the mall this weekend too."

"Great!" said Stephanie, smiling along with them. It had worked! The Jennifers were impressed.

Now she had only one tiny problem. Her dad had said she was still too young to get her ears pierced! What was she going to do?

THREE

When the Jennifers left, Stephanie knew
she needed some help. And D.J. was the perfect person to help her. Glancing out a window, she saw that her sister and Steve weren't
in the yard. So Stephanie hurried down the
hall to her sister's room. The door was half
open, and she could see that D.J. was doing
homework with Steve and her best friend,
Kimmy.

"Rules," D.J. reminded Stephanie when she

walked into the room. Stephanie stepped back outside and knocked. "Enter," said D.J.

"D.J., will you take me down to the mall?" Stephanie asked. "I have to get my ears pierced."

"I can't," D.J. replied, not looking up from her notebook. "You have to have a parent with you. Ask Dad."

"Dad?" Stephanie yelped. "He won't even let me put holes in my jeans." With a loud sigh, Stephanie flopped onto D.J.'s bed. This was a disaster!

"What's the big deal about getting your ears pierced?" Steve asked. "My dad did it to try to be hip, but he just looked like a pirate accountant."

Stephanie looked at Steve. He was cute, but sometimes he didn't make much sense. "Thanks, you're a real comfort," she said.

"Hey, I do my best." He laughed. "Well, Deej, I have to get going now. I've got wrestling practice."

D.J. got up from her desk. "I'll walk you downstairs," she offered.

"You know, squirt," Kimmy said when Steve

and D.J. were gone. "I can pierce your ears for you."

Stephanie immediately sat up on the bed. "You can?"

Kimmy nodded. "My brother, Garth, works at the Piercing Palace. I can have him bring home the gun."

"Gun? What gun?" Stephanie asked in alarm. She didn't like the sound of that one bit.

"An ear gun," Kimmy explained. "There's nothing to it. I've seen my brother do it a hundred times." Kimmy got up and formed a gun shape with her thumb and forefinger. "It's easy," she said, pointing her finger gun at Stephanie. "You just point the gun and . . . *pow*!" Kimmy reeled backward as if there'd been a huge explosion.

Stephanie shook her head slowly. What had she been thinking? She couldn't let Kimmy pierce her ears. Kimmy was the biggest goof-up around. Anything Kimmy touched turned into a mess. "Like I *might* let you near me with a weapon," Stephanie told her. "Your parents don't even let you use a fork."

Kimmy shrugged. "Suit yourself, clip-on queen."

Right then, Stephanie spotted her dad going down the hall with the twins. *Maybe he'll change his mind*, she thought. It was worth a try, anyway. Stephanie was desperate.

Stephanie hopped off the bed and ran out into the hall. "Dad," she called to him.

Her dad turned to her as the twins went down the stairs on their behinds. "What is it, sweetie?"

Stephanie took a deep breath for courage. "Can we go to the mall tonight?" she asked.

"Sure," he said with a smile.

"Can we get frozen yogurt?" Stephanie asked.

"I'll even spring for a waffle cone," Danny said. *He's in a good mood*, Stephanie noted. That was a good sign.

"Great," said Stephanie. "So, we'll get frozen yogurt, get my shoes fixed, get my ears pierced, and get a new headband."

"Whoa!" said her father. "Back up a little."

"Get my shoes fixed?" Stephanie asked, knowing full well that wasn't what he meant.

"After that," said Danny.

"Get a new headband?"

"Before that."

Stephanie tried to act casual, as if what she was about to say were no big deal. "Oh, you must mean get my ears pierced."

"That's the one," said Danny.

"So, let's get going," said Stephanie brightly. "We want to get a good parking spot."

"Forget it, Steph. You're too young," said Danny.

Stephanie's shoulders sagged in disappointment. "But Jennifer got hers pierced," she argued.

"Well, I'm not her father," he said firmly.

"But Jennifer got hers pierced," Stephanie said.

"You said that already," Danny pointed out.

"There are two Jennifers," Stephanie reminded him. "Four ears, all pierced."

Her dad bent down so he was looking her right in the eye. "Listen, Steph. D.J. got her ears pierced in eighth grade. When you get to eighth grade, you can get yours pierced too."

Stephanie stamped her foot angrily. "But

I'm not D.J.!"

"Sorry, I don't make the rules," said Danny. Then he thought about that a minute and realized it wasn't true. "Actually, I do make the rules. And I happen to think this is a good one," he said.

"You are so unfair!" Stephanie shouted. "How am I ever going to be cool?"

"What are you talking about?" Danny asked. "I just got you those neat new sunglasses."

Sunglasses? Stephanie didn't even want to think about those! The Jennifers had thought she was a total dweeb when she'd shown them the glasses! Dad just didn't understand. He was hopelessly old-fashioned and out of touch. Stephanie turned and stomped back into D.J.'s room.

"I guess that didn't go too well," said Kimmy, looking up from her homework.

"It sure didn't," Stephanie said. "Kimmy, how soon can you get that ear-gun thing?"

"If I can catch Garth before he leaves work, I could have it tonight."

Stephanie picked up D.J.'s phone. "Give him a call, okay?"

"You got it," said Kimmy, dialing the mall. After she spoke with her brother, she told Stephanie, "He'll bring it home tonight."

"All right!" Stephanie cheered. "Thanks, Kimmy."

"No problemo," Kimmy said, going back to her homework.

Stephanie's smile slowly faded. She hated to disobey her father like this. Most of the time he tried to be fair. But he just didn't understand that she wasn't D.J. The things that were right for D.J. weren't necessarily right for her. Why couldn't he see that?

She stretched out on her stomach on D.J.'s bed and plunked her chin onto her hands. She couldn't get over the uncomfortable feeling that she was somehow hurting her father by disobeying him. She wasn't, though—was she? After all, they were *her* ears. *She* was the one who needed to have them pierced, not him. A person should be able to decide what to do about her own ears, she decided.

Just then, D.J. came back in the room. Stephanie wasn't sure whether or not to tell her sister her plan. D.J. might try to talk her out of it, and Stephanie didn't want to be talked out of it. She decided to keep quiet.

Stephanie felt nervous all through supper that night. Would the piercing hurt? Did Kimmy really know what she was doing? What would happen if her father noticed her ears were pierced?

She was quiet as she helped clear the table and stack the dishwasher. "Are you okay, Steph?" asked Becky.

"Oh, just fine," she said, trying to sound normal. Finally, at seven o'clock, Kimmy knocked on the back door. It was perfect timing. D.J. had gone out on a date with Steve. Joey and Uncle Jesse were still down at the radio station. The twins were asleep. And Dad and Becky were sitting on the front porch talking about their TV show. No one would even know Kimmy was there.

"Have you got the thing?" Stephanie asked in a secretive voice.

"Right here," Kimmy said, nodding toward the brown paper bag she was holding.

They hurried upstairs into Stephanie's room. "Out, Michelle," Stephanie said when she saw that Michelle was there playing on the floor with Comet, the family dog.

Michelle shook her head. "No way. I have a guest."

Stephanie put her hands on her hips. "Your guest drinks out of the toilet."

Michelle looked up at Kimmy. "So does yours."

Kimmy made a face at Michelle. Michelle made a face back. "Michelle, Kimmy and I have something important to do," said Stephanie.

Michelle looked up sharply at Stephanie. "Something important? Well, well." She remembered the talk they'd had in the kitchen that afternoon. "You made me a promise, Stephanie, when I gave you your privacy with the Jennifers. You said you'd let me stay in the room the next time something important was happening."

"Michelle," Stephanie pleaded.

"You promised," Michelle reminded her. "If it's something important, I get to stay."

"Let the runt stay," said Kimmy. "I work better with an audience."

It didn't seem to Stephanie that she had much choice. "Okay," she said, giving in. "But whatever goes on in this room is top secret." She held out her pinky to Michelle. "Pinky-swear."

Michelle held out her pinky. "Wow! Pinky-swear. This is big." Michelle and Stephanie locked pinkies and shook. Then Stephanie brushed her hair back into a ponytail.

"Okay," said Kimmy. "Park your lobes right here."

Stephanie sat on a chair as Kimmy took the metal ear gun from the bag. It looked like a large silver stapler. Stephanie gulped nervously when she saw it.

Michelle didn't like the look of it either. "What's that?" she asked.

"It's an ear gun," Stephanie explained. "Dad wouldn't let me get my ears pierced, so I'm letting Kimmy do it."

Michelle's eyes went wide. "Are you *nuts*?"

"No, I'm desperate," Stephanie replied.

Michelle didn't think this sounded like a good idea. But there was nothing she could do about it. "Okay . . ." she said, her voice trailing off doubtfully.

"Let's rock and roll!" Kimmy sang out.

"Are you sure you know how to use that thing?" Stephanie asked.

"Hey, do I get D's in English?" Kimmy said confidently.

Stephanie took that reply to mean yes. "Go ahead," she said.

Kimmy loaded the ear gun with a small, gold ball earring. She held it to Stephanie's ear and said, "Here goes . . ." With a quick click and pinch, the earring was snapped into Stephanie's ear. "Hey, that wasn't too bad," said Stephanie.

"Yeah, I'm a crack shot," Kimmy said proudly. "I practiced on some cold cuts before I came over." She loaded another earring into the gun and did Stephanie's other ear. Then she turned to Michelle. "You next? How about a nice nose ring?"

"I'm out of here," said Michelle, hopping off the bed. She ran out of the room with Comet trailing behind her.

"Well, I'd better take these things out before Dad sees them," Stephanie said as she looked in the mirror.

Stephanie began to take out the earrings, but Kimmy grabbed her hand. "Hold it. You have to leave those studs in for at least six weeks, until your ears heal."

"*Six weeks*?" Stephanie cried. "I can't do that! I was only going to wear them to school to impress my friends. If I wear them around here, I'll be in big trouble."

"If you take them out now, they'll heal right up and you won't have holes in your ears," Kimmy told her.

Stephanie sighed deeply and plopped onto her bed. What a problem! If she took the earrings out, the Jennifers would never invite her to sit at their table. If she left them in, she would get into really big trouble with her father. "I'm dead meat," she muttered. "Dead meat."

FOUR

Stephanie pulled a pocket mirror from her backpack and checked her hair. Her blond waves were pulled down tightly over her ears and clipped in the back. The gold ball earring in her right ear had popped through her hair. She quickly tucked it back under.

It was Tuesday, and she'd gotten through the entire weekend and Monday without anyone at home knowing about her earrings. She'd been very careful to keep the earrings hidden under her hair.

Although she'd been successful at hiding her earrings from her family, she'd been *un*successful in showing them to the Jennifers. All day Monday she'd tried to get their attention. But each time she approached them, they acted like they didn't see her. They moved away or began talking to someone else.

Were they avoiding her? Had their Friday visit convinced them that she was a hopeless dweeb?

Maybe they really hadn't seen her each time she'd gone up to them. Maybe she was being too sensitive.

Somehow Stephanie doubted it. Her clip-ons had turned the Jennifers completely against her. As long as they thought she wore clip-ons, they would never invite her to sit at their cool table.

Stephanie knew her only hope was to show them her pierced ears. That was the one way she could regain their respect. She would just have to get their attention.

She would have to wait a bit longer, though. First she had to go to the elementary school to help with the second-grade play. She'd gotten special permission from her English teacher to take the time off from school.

As much as she was looking forward to the play, she wished the rehearsal wasn't today. It was hard to think about the play when she was dying to show the Jennifers her ears.

There was another problem, too. Joey and Uncle Jesse would be there. She couldn't let them see her earrings. They'd be sure to mention it to her father. And she couldn't pinky-swear *them* to secrecy!

Stephanie walked into the elementary school and straight to the auditorium. All the kids in Michelle's class, plus kids from the two other second-grade classes, were already there. Some kids sat cross-legged on the stage floor. Others were running around the stage chasing each other and yelling.

Joey and Uncle Jesse were on the stage with the second graders. The two guys looked sort of confused and helpless as the kids chattered and goofed around. Stephanie could see they needed her help in getting things under control.

She tossed her backpack onto a chair and

walked up the side steps onto the stage. Clapping her hands sharply for attention, she shouted, "Okay, kids, I'm Ms. Tanner!" Stephanie continued in a no-nonsense voice. "I will be your choreographer. This is Mr. Joey Gladstone and Mr. Jesse Katsopolis. I've asked them to direct."

Stephanie could see her firm tone was working. The kids had all settled down and were listening to her. Even Michelle was paying close attention.

"Now, you're going to work," Stephanie told them. "And you're going to sweat. When I say 'Jump,' you're going to say 'How high?' Got it?"

"Thank you, Steph," said Joey, stepping forward. "I think Jesse and I can take it from here."

Michelle got up and walked over to Stephanie. "Hi, Michelle," said Stephanie. "Are you ready to audition?"

Michelle nodded.

"Remember what we worked on," Stephanie whispered to her. Stephanie had worked with Michelle the entire weekend. She had taught her little sister to sing "Yankee Doodle" exactly as she'd sung it when she played the part in the second grade—and exactly as D.J. had taught her.

Michelle put her hand on Stephanie's arm. "Your earring is showing," she said softly.

"My earring!" Stephanie gasped. She looked sharply at Joey and Uncle Jesse as she tucked in the earring. They didn't seem to have noticed.

"And one more thing," Michelle added.

"What?" asked Stephanie.

"Try not to get too power crazy," Michelle requested. "I have to go to school with these kids. They all know you're my sister. I don't want them to hate me."

Stephanie frowned. "Thank you, Michelle," she said in a stern voice for everyone to hear. "Now please take your seat with the other students."

Michelle went back and sat down next to a classmate named Denise. "Your sister is already getting on my nerves," Denise whispered to Michelle.

Michelle smiled. "Try living with her."

"Okay, kids," said Joey. "We're here to have a good time."

"We're going to sing, we're going to dance, we're going to put on a great show," Uncle Jesse added, doing a little dance step and twirling around quickly.

A second grader named Aaron Bailey spoke up. "So far, we're just sitting here."

Joey patted the boy on the back and said, "You've got to take time off once in a while, Aaron. Okay, let's start the auditions."

Uncle Jesse sat down at the piano and played. One by one, each of the kids got up and sang "Yankee Doodle."

Michelle watched nervously. Some of the kids were pretty good. But so far she hadn't seen anyone she thought was better than she was.

When her turn came, Michelle got up and gave it all she had. She sang loudly, and even dropped to one knee and stuck out her arms dramatically at the end.

"Very good!" Stephanie cried, applauding. Then she remembered she wasn't supposed to show any favoritism toward her sister. "I mean, very nice, Ms. Tanner. Take your seat, please," she added seriously.

Michelle gave Stephanie a small smile and walked away from the piano. As she took her place back on the floor, the other kids were smiling, nodding, and giving her the thumbs-up sign.

When all the kids had auditioned, Joey and Uncle Jesse got together at the back of the auditorium so they could discuss the auditions privately.

"Okay, quiet down," Uncle Jesse told the kids as he walked back onto the stage. "Here's a list of who will be playing what part. George Washington will be played by"—he paused for drama—"Aaron Bailey."

"Do I have the biggest part?" Aaron asked excitedly.

"You have the biggest mouth," Uncle Jesse quipped under his breath.

Joey stepped forward. "And Denise Frazier will play his wife, Martha Washington."

Denise and Aaron looked at each other with disgust. It was clear they didn't like the idea of being married, even in a play. "*Ewww!*" they both said at once.

"And now for the very important part of Yankee Doodle," said Joey.

Michelle sucked in her breath. Denise pinched her arm lightly. "That's going to be you," she assured Michelle in a whisper.

"And the part of Yankee Doodle goes to . . ." Joey said again, building the suspense.

But before he could announce the name, a dark-haired boy sitting behind most of the other kids shot his hand into the air.

"Yes, son," said Uncle Jesse. "You can go to the bathroom."

"Excuse me, but I didn't get a chance to try out," said the boy. Michelle looked at him sharply. She knew his name was Derek and he was in one of the other second grades.

"Oh, we're sorry," said Joey. "We didn't see you way back there."

"That's okay," said Derek in a small voice. "I tend to blend in with my surroundings."

Stephanie knew that was true. Although she didn't know him well, she knew he was a shy kid. She remembered him from the year before, when she'd still been in the elementary school and he'd been in first grade. He'd sat quietly every day in the cafeteria with his one and only friend.

"Well, we want to give everyone a chance," said Uncle Jesse. "Come on up to the piano."

Stephanie tried not to feel too annoyed at the delay. There wasn't much chance that shy Derek was going to win the part. This was just a waste of time. Still, she understood that it was only fair to give him a chance.

Derek stood next to the piano and straightened his shoulders. "In the key of E, please," he said to Uncle Jesse.

Stephanie's jaw fell as Derek went into his act. Not only did he sing in a full, beautiful voice, but he could also tap-dance! Derek sang and tap-danced like a professional.

The other kids looked as stunned as Stephanie did. No one could believe it!

When he was done, the kids all clapped and cheered. Joey and Uncle Jesse rushed over to Derek. "That was unbelievable!" Joey cried.

"Incredible!" agreed Uncle Jesse. "We've found our Yankee Doodle." He and Joey slapped high-fives with Derek. All the kids crowded around him excitedly.

Only Stephanie noticed Michelle sitting alone, her eyes brimming with tears of disappointment.

FIVE

That afternoon, Michelle walked into the house in a very bad mood. She'd been betrayed by her own family. How much worse could things get?

Her dad jumped up from the couch when he saw her. But he didn't seem to notice the pout on her face or the way she had stomped into the room. "So, Michelle," he said happily, "how's the star of the second-grade play?"

Stephanie came in the door right behind

Michelle. She cringed when she heard her dad's words.

"Why don't you go to his house and ask him," Michelle grumbled as she wiggled out of her backpack.

Her dad frowned with concern. "What happened?"

"Uncle Jesse and Joey picked someone else," Stephanie told her dad.

"What?" Danny gasped.

Joey and Uncle Jesse were coming down the stairs just then. "Michelle was great, but Derek was greater," Joey explained.

"I'm sorry Stephanie got your hopes up, Michelle," said Uncle Jesse apologetically. "After the audition she told us how you were hoping to be Yankee Doodle. But we told you at school, Michelle, we have to be fair."

Michelle didn't want to hear their excuses. "Why?" she demanded.

"Well, honey," said Danny, "if someone really was better, then Jesse and Joey did the right thing, and you have to accept that."

Oh, great! Michelle thought angrily. *Now Dad's even taking their side.* What was going on? Had her entire family turned against her? They all used to stick up for one another.

"But don't worry, munchkin," said Uncle Jesse. "We still have a great part for you."

"You're on the stage the whole time and you're the center of everything," Joey added.

This was starting to sound interesting. Michelle folded her arms and looked at them warily. "I'm listening," she said.

"Lady Liberty!" Uncle Jesse announced with a big smile.

"The Statue of Liberty?" Michelle cried unhappily, throwing her arms up in disgust. "Statues can't talk or sing. They can't dance either."

"This one does," said Joey. "We made up the part just for you. So we can have her do anything we want her to do. And we've written a line in for you, too."

"What is it?" asked Michelle.

"I'm Lady Liberty," Joey said.

"That's it?" Michelle asked in disbelief.

"It's a very important line," said Uncle Jesse.

With tears in her eyes, Michelle stormed up the stairs.

Stephanie felt so sorry for Michelle. She knew how much getting the part meant to her. She also knew Derek had been the right choice.

"I'd better go talk to her," said Stephanie. She ran up the stairs and found her sister sulking in their room.

"Please leave me alone," said Michelle. "I'm in a very bad mood."

"I'm not in such a good mood either," Stephanie admitted as she sat on the bed next to Michelle.

"Why? What's the matter with you?" Michelle asked.

"It's my ears. They hurt, and they're really red." Just after rehearsal, Stephanie had noticed a burning sensation in her earlobes. As the day went on it had gotten worse and worse. Right now, Stephanie's ears felt like they were on fire.

Stephanie unclipped her hair and tucked the strands behind her ears. "I think they're infected," she told Michelle.

Michelle inspected Stephanie's earlobes. They were so red and puffy, it hurt just to look at them. *Stephanie should have known better than to let Kimmy near them*, Michelle thought. But she wasn't in the mood to be too sympathetic. "Oh, no!" she cried. "Are they going to fall off?"

"Of course not," Stephanie snapped irritably. "They just hurt—a lot."

"Good, because your head would look really weird," said Michelle. She knew she wasn't being very helpful, but she was in such a bad mood!

Stephanie didn't feel like putting up with Michelle's silly remarks. Her ears hurt too much. "Michelle, just drop it, okay?"

But Michelle didn't feel like dropping it. Stephanie had sided with Joey and Uncle Jesse. She was the choreographer, so she could have at least tried to talk them out of giving Derek the part. "And how would you keep your reading glasses on?" Michelle went on.

"I'll glue them to my nose, okay?" Stephanie said impatiently. "Now remember, you pinky-swore you wouldn't tell Dad."

"Okay, okay, I won't tell. But if your ears

fall off, do I get your Walkman?"

Stephanie had had enough of Michelle's teasing. "Listen, Michelle. I didn't come up here to talk about my ears. I just wanted you to know you're not the only one with problems. I really came up to talk to you about the play. Joey and Uncle Jesse did the only thing that was fair. Derek is . . . like . . . a supertalent. They had to pick him."

"What am I? A nothing?" Michelle sulked.

"No, you're Lady Liberty. It's a very important part. What if I make up a little dance for you to do?"

Michelle crossed her arms. "A statue dancing? That's stupid."

"Calling a feather macaroni is stupid, too. But that doesn't bother anyone," Stephanie insisted.

"You don't get it, do you?" said Michelle. "I wouldn't even mind being the dumb old statue, except that . . . except that . . ."

"Except what?" Stephanie prodded.

"Except that you and D.J. were Yankee Doodle!" Michelle exploded.

"What does that matter?" Stephanie asked.

"It means I'm not as good as you and D.J.," Michelle muttered, looking down at the floor.

"Of course you are," said Stephanie. "We weren't up against a mega-talent like Derek. That kid is, like, the next Michael Jackson."

Stephanie could see her words weren't helping Michelle, who just kept looking at the floor. "Come on, Michelle, cheer up," Stephanie pressed.

"I don't want to talk about it anymore," said Michelle in a sad voice. "I don't even want to think about it."

"Suit yourself," Stephanie said with a sigh. She got off Michelle's bed and went over to her own.

Maybe doing homework would keep her mind off her burning earlobes. She took her history book from her backpack, but it was hard to pay attention to it with her ears hurting so much.

Before supper that night, Stephanie clipped her hair back once again so it covered her ears. Just as she was about to go into the kitchen, Michelle tapped her on the back. Stephanie turned around.

"Your earring is peeking through your hair again," Michelle whispered.

"Thanks," said Stephanie, tucking the earring back under her hair. She'd have to come up with a new hairdo for covering her ears. She couldn't count on this one to be foolproof.

She ate supper quickly. It was strange how painful earlobes could kill a person's appetite. Besides that, she was too worried about her dad spotting the earrings to enjoy her meal.

After supper, she went straight back to her bedroom. Feeling very grumpy, she pulled some old magazines out from under her bed. They were movie magazines that had once belonged to D.J. Stephanie liked to look at them, especially the ones that showed photos of the *Star Wars* movies. Stephanie had the complete video collection of *Star Wars* and watched it a lot.

As she was flipping through the magazine, a picture of the actress Carrie Fisher playing Princess Leah caught her eye. Princess Leah wore her hair in two thick coils of braids, one over either ear.

"That's it!" Stephanie cried. It would be a

perfect hairstyle for covering her own ears. Not a bit of ear showed!

The next morning, Stephanie got up early to work on her new hairstyle. She made a braid on either side and wrapped each braid in a circle over her ears. It took a lot of hairpins to make the coils of hair stay in place. And her coils were droopier than Princess Leah's coils. But it looked okay. The important thing was that her ears were completely hidden.

Stephanie was glad she'd thought of wearing her hair this way. By now her ears were redder than they'd been the day before. They'd be even harder to hide.

When she went downstairs to the kitchen, her dad and Michelle were already there. "Hey, Steph, interesting hairdo," he said as he took a container of milk from the refrigerator. "What's that, the *Star Wars* look?"

"Uh . . . yeah," Stephanie stammered. "We're doing a 'Hairstyles of the Seventies' thing at school today, and I'm going as Princess Leah."

"Really?" said Danny with a smile. "I feel

sorry for the kid going as Kojak."

"Who's that?" asked Michelle, pouring a bowl of cereal.

"He was a detective on TV who was bald," Danny explained.

Stephanie smiled weakly. She didn't know how she would get through the day. Her ears hurt so much she felt like she was losing her mind.

SIX

"And keep in step," Stephanie told the kids that day in rehearsal. They were all dancing in a line, doing the steps she'd taught them. And doing them badly.

Some kids were kicking one way. Other kids were going in the opposite direction. They bumped into one another. In some spots they were so bunched up they looked as if they were about to tumble over one another like a line of dominos.

Stephanie couldn't stand to watch them. They were going to disgrace the Tanner family. After all, this was a Tanner (and Gladstone and Katsopolis) family production.

Over in the corner, Uncle Jesse played the piano. Off to the side of the dancing kids, Michelle was holding up her Lady Liberty torch, which was made from a cardboard paper-towel roll wrapped in aluminum foil. Joey stood nearby with his arms folded, keeping an eye on everything. The family honor was at stake here. These kids were going to make fools of them.

"Come on, kids," Stephanie coached desperately. She clapped to the beat as she said, "One-two, one-two, one-two . . ."

It was a bad situation. No matter what she did, the kids were hopelessly, completely out of step. They looked absolutely terrible!

"Stop! Cut! Nobody move!" Stephanie screamed at them. Her red, burning ears made it even harder to have patience. "Okay, everybody. Apparently we're going to have to go right back to the basics of dancing." Stephanie held up her right foot and shook it.

"This is a foot!"

"Okay, why don't we take a little break from dancing," Joey cut in.

From the way Joey glanced at her, Stephanie realized she was being too rough with the kids. Maybe it wasn't really their fault. It was her ears. They were turning her into a total crab!

Not only did they hurt like crazy, but she couldn't show them to the Jennifers now. They were so red and puffy, they looked disgusting. There was absolutely nothing cool about them!

Now she had to hide them from her family and the Jennifers. Her only hope was that she could hang on until her ears got better (assuming they ever would). Then she could unveil them to the Jennifers and win her rightful spot among the cool kids. Until then, she was sidelined with red, puffy ears.

"Why don't we take it from George Washington's line," Joey suggested, looking over to Aaron.

Aaron stood straight and stepped toward the front of the stage as he recited his line: "A proud symbol welcomes all to our country and reminds us that we are free."

Aaron and all the students then turned toward Michelle as they were supposed to at that point in the play. They waited for her to speak her line, but Michelle didn't say anything.

"Michelle, you have a line," Joey reminded her. "I am Lady Liberty."

Michelle glared at him. "I am Lady Liberty . . . I should have been Yankee Doodle!"

At that, Uncle Jesse stood up from behind the piano. "Okay. Take five, kids."

The second graders all stared at him blankly. They had never heard the expression "take five."

"Just take a break," said Uncle Jesse.

Right away, the kids began talking and running around the stage. Joey, Uncle Jesse, and Stephanie went over to talk to Michelle.

"What's wrong, Michelle?" asked Uncle Jesse.

"My arm's getting bored," said Michelle, rubbing the arm that had been holding the torch. "I don't want to be the Statue of Liberty."

"Maybe we can write her a little song-and-dance number," Joey suggested to Uncle Jesse.

"I already offered," said Stephanie, "but she thinks it's dumb for a statue to dance."

"It *is* dumb," Michelle insisted.

"I think so too," Uncle Jesse agreed. "Besides, we can't spoil her like that, Joey. She needs to learn to be a team player."

Joey nodded. "I guess you're right."

"Michelle," said Uncle Jesse. "If you don't want to be the Statue of Liberty, then you can sit down there and watch with the other kids."

Michelle couldn't believe what she was hearing. "Fine!" she snapped at him. Then she stomped off the stage and took a seat in the front row of the auditorium. She was so mad at Uncle Jesse and Joey. *I might never forgive them!* she thought.

"All right, come on, kids," Uncle Jesse said, clapping his hands for attention. "We've got a show to do." Michelle watched as the rehearsal went on from there without Lady Liberty. That only made Michelle feel worse. Her part wasn't important at all. They could do very well without her.

After school and all through dinner, Michelle didn't speak one word to Uncle Jesse or Joey. She'd made up her mind never to speak to them again.

After dinner, she wasn't in the mood to see anyone. She went up to her room and took out a coloring book. Michelle liked to color when she was angry. It felt good to press really hard with the crayon, and maybe even make a mess of the picture.

She was coloring a tree a deep purple when she heard a knock on the door. She looked up and saw the last people on earth she wanted to see. Uncle Jesse and Joey were standing in her bedroom doorway. "Hi, pumpkin," said Uncle Jesse.

Michelle took her book to her bed and flopped onto it. She went back to her coloring, not even looking at Joey and Uncle Jesse.

"Oh, I get it," Uncle Jesse said. "You're not talking to us." He turned to Joey. "She's not talking to us."

"Are you sure?" Joey asked. "Michelle, are you not talking to us?"

Michelle nodded but still didn't look at

either of them.

"She's not talking to us," Joey said to Uncle Jesse.

"Okay, all those who are ticked off at Joey and Uncle Jesse say I," said Uncle Jesse.

Michelle shot her hand into the air. "I!" Suddenly she realized they'd gotten her to speak. "Hey, you tricked me!"

"I know," said Uncle Jesse as he stepped into her room. "You think we've been unfair. Right?"

"Right," Michelle said with a nod.

"Well, we think you're being unfair," Uncle Jesse said.

Michelle was surprised. She hadn't expected him to say that! She'd expected "Sorry" or "We beg you to forgive us."

"Michelle, everyone in that play is working really hard," said Joey, sitting on the end of her bed. "If we don't have a Statue of Liberty, you'll be letting down all the other kids. Is that what you want?"

Michelle didn't like the way this little talk was going. Were they trying to confuse her? Well, she wouldn't let them. "No, I want to be

Yankee Doodle like Stephanie and D.J.," she said.

"I'm sorry, but we don't always get what we want in life," said Joey. He thought about this a moment and then added, "When I was a little boy, I wanted to be Fred Flintstone, but I had too many toes."

Uncle Jesse made a face at him for being so silly. "Excuse me a minute, Michelle," he said. Then he playfully smacked Joey on the arm.

Michelle had to bite down on her laughter. Joey and Uncle Jesse always made her laugh. That was one of the things she loved about them. But right now she was mad, and she was determined to stay mad.

Uncle Jesse turned back to her. "Michelle, it's like being in a band. Not everyone can be the lead singer."

"You are," Michelle reminded him. How could Uncle Jesse understand how she felt? He was *always* the lead singer in every band he was ever in.

"Yeah, but I'm no more important than the bass player," he argued. "You know the bass player . . . what's his name? The guy with the long, curly hair. Larry? Lenny?"

Michelle folded her arms. Uncle Jesse wasn't exactly making her feel better.

"Okay, bad example," Uncle Jesse admitted.

"Excuse me, Michelle," said Joey. Then he smacked Uncle Jesse back for making such a bad argument. Then Joey turned to Michelle. "What Jesse is trying to say is that you're part of a team. And everyone has to do his or her share."

"Exactly," Uncle Jesse agreed. "And believe me, my band wouldn't be as good without Larry or Lenny . . . what is that guy's name?"

"The point is," Joey cut in quickly, "a lot of people are counting on you."

"So, you want to go out there and be the best Statue of Liberty you can be," said Uncle Jesse. "Got it?"

"Got it," Michelle agreed. In her heart, she knew they were right. "And his name is Lanny," she told Uncle Jesse.

"Aha!" Uncle Jesse said.

Uncle Jesse and Joey both kissed Michelle on the head and left. Michelle flopped back onto her bed. They were right, she realized.

And maybe she had been acting like a brat. Just because D.J. and Stephanie had been Yankee Doodle, she didn't have to be. She wasn't either one of her sisters—she was herself. Besides, neither of them had ever been Lady Liberty. Didn't that make *her* special? She decided then and there that she would be the best Lady Liberty the school had ever seen.

SEVEN

Just before bedtime, Stephanie uncoiled her hair and looked at her ears in the mirror. Although they'd burned all day long, they now felt like a five-alarm blaze. She half expected to see smoke coming out of them.

Stephanie couldn't remember *ever* feeling this miserable in her entire life!

Just then the door opened. In walked Michelle with D.J. right behind her. "See," said Michelle to D.J. "I told you her ears look like Frankenberries."

Stephanie was too surprised to even move. D.J. came alongside her and gazed at her ears. She made a pained face. "Stephanie, your ears are infected!"

"Michelle, you promised you wouldn't tell," Stephanie said angrily.

"I promised I wouldn't tell *Dad*," Michelle reminded her. "Does this look like Dad?"

Gingerly, D.J. touched Stephanie's right ear. To Stephanie, it felt as if D.J. had stuck a knife in her earlobe. "Ow!" she howled in pain.

"Did you pierce them at the mall after Dad told you not to?" D.J. asked.

"Of course not," Stephanie said, turning away from D.J. "I'm not that stupid!"

"She let Kimmy do it," Michelle told D.J.

D.J.'s jaw dropped. "What? You let *Kimmy* punch a hole in your body? Why didn't you just fall on a rusty nail? Steph, you've got to tell Dad. He needs to take you to a doctor."

"No way!" Stephanie said firmly. She could *not* tell her dad. She'd rather suffer the unbearable burning in her earlobes.

"The doctor isn't so bad," said Michelle. "If

you don't yell, you get a lollipop. And if you yell a lot, you get two."

"Come on, Stephanie," D.J. urged her. "If you don't tell him, I will."

"You wouldn't!" Stephanie cried, shocked.

"Normally, I wouldn't," D.J. agreed. "But this is serious. I can't let you fool around with your health."

Stephanie's shoulders sagged in defeat. She had no choice now. "Oh, all right," she said with a sigh. "I'll tell him tomorrow." It would be better if she told her father instead of D.J. telling him.

"Dad's doing a crossword puzzle down in the living room," D.J. told her. "You might as well get it over with."

"You mean right now?" Stephanie gulped.

D.J. nodded. "It's you or me, kiddo."

"Okay," Stephanie agreed. "Will you come with me?"

"Sure," D.J. said. Slowly, Stephanie left her room with D.J. behind her.

"Good luck!" Michelle called down the hall after them.

Together they went down the stairs. Just as

D.J. had said, their dad had a magazine on his knee and was working hard at the crossword puzzle on the last page.

He was so involved with the puzzle that Stephanie and D.J. got all the way to the side of the couch and he still didn't notice them. "Let's see," he spoke out loud to himself. "A defunct Russian philosophy . . . twelve letters . . . starting with c-z-f . . . czf-ism . . . nah."

D.J. cleared her throat to get his attention. Startled, he jumped a little when he realized they were standing there.

"Sorry, Dad," said Stephanie. "I see you're in the middle of something important." Losing her nerve, she turned to leave. But D.J. gently caught her by the shoulders and turned her back around. "Okay, okay," Stephanie muttered.

"What is it, Stephanie?" her father asked.

"Dad, before you get angry . . ." Stephanie began.

Danny's face fell. "I hate conversations that begin like that," he said.

Stephanie nodded. "Me too. See you," she said as she turned and began walking away.

Once again, D.J. reached out and caught Stephanie by the shoulders. This time she kept her arm around Stephanie as she walked her back toward their dad. "Dad, Stephanie did an incredibly stupid thing," D.J. told him calmly. "But there's a reason for it. Keep in mind that she's at an age where life can be terribly confusing. And—"

"Can we get back to the incredibly stupid thing?" Danny interrupted.

Stephanie knew there was no point in beating around the bush any longer. The awful moment of truth had come. "Dad, I let Kimmy Gibbler pierce my ears!" she blurted out. She waited for her dad's reaction.

Danny smiled in disbelief. "Yeah, right. C'mon, what did you really do?"

He wasn't making this easy. Stephanie would just have to show him. She pulled her hair away from her ears and watched her dad go pale with shock. "You're serious!" he cried. "Do you know how dangerous that is?"

"Just remember, Dad," D.J. jumped in. "Stephanie's only 11. I mean, I've made a lot of dumb mistakes in my time. Things you wouldn't even believe."

That caught their dad's attention. "Like what?" he asked.

D.J. obviously realized she'd said too much. She backed away, waving her hands. "Uh . . . Maybe you two should work this out without me." With that, she made a beeline up the stairs.

Stephanie didn't really blame her. There was no sense in the two of them getting into trouble.

Danny turned his attention back to Stephanie. She hated the hurt look on his face. This was even worse than getting yelled at.

"Stephanie, you lied to me and deliberately disobeyed me," he said. "I told you, you could pierce your ears when you got to eighth grade like D.J."

"Why do I have to do everything like D.J.?" Stephanie asked. "I'm not D.J.; I'm me. I want to be treated like an individual."

"Okay," Danny said thoughtfully. "Good point."

"It is?" Stephanie said, surprised. She hadn't expected him to agree. Then she realized she should keep talking as long as he was agreeing with her. "I mean, it is. Yes, it is."

"But let me ask you a question," said Danny. "Why exactly did you want your ears pierced?"

"All my friends have them," Stephanie replied.

"So . . . you want to be an individual, but you still want to be exactly like your friends?"

"Well, no. I guess . . . maybe."

"If your friends didn't have pierced ears, would you still want them?" Danny asked.

"I don't know," Stephanie admitted with a shrug. "Is this a trick question?"

"Stephanie, if you want to be an individual, you have to know what you want. As you get older, you're going to be making more and more tough decisions. And you don't make them based on what your friends are doing, or what's popular, or what you see on TV. You have to decide what's best for you."

"How will I know?" Stephanie asked.

"You think about what's right," Danny answered. "And if there's ever any doubt, that's what I'm here for. I love you, Steph."

"I love you too, Dad. I'm sorry." Stephanie put her arms around her dad and hugged him. He hugged back, holding her tight.

When the hug ended, Danny kept his hand on Stephanie's shoulder. "I'll tell you what," he said. "From now on, we look at each situation and base the rules on what works for you."

"That sounds great," Stephanie said with a smile.

"And I'd better get you to a doctor to look at those ears," he added.

"Good idea," Stephanie agreed. She felt so relieved. That hadn't been too bad. And now her ears were going to be treated. No more sizzling lobes. D.J. had been right. Telling Dad was the best thing to do.

"Then we'll stop for a burger and fries," said Danny as he went to the hall closet and got his jacket.

"Dad, you're on a roll," Stephanie said happily.

"Which is the best meal you'll have for a long time," Danny added.

Stephanie's face fell. She knew exactly what

he meant. "Grounded, huh?"

Danny nodded.

"I should have seen that coming," said Stephanie. "But what about the school play?"

"That's a part of school, so you can still work on that."

Stephanie took her jacket from the closet. "All right." At least if her ears were better, she'd have more patience with the kids. All in all, things hadn't turned out *too* badly.

EIGHT

Stephanie peeked out from behind the stage curtain. It was the afternoon of the big show. The auditorium was filling up fast. She spotted her dad and Becky taking a seat, with D.J. and Steve following them.

Joey came up alongside her. "How are the old ears doing?" he asked.

"They're better," Stephanie said with a smile. It had been over a week since she'd been to the doctor. The doctor had removed the earrings and given her an antibiotic ointment to put on them. Now her ears no longer burned. The holes would close up as they healed. She wouldn't have pierced ears—at least not yet—but that no longer seemed as important as it had. The Jennifers would have to like her as she was, clip-on earrings and all. And if they didn't, it was their loss.

"Okay, showtime," Joey told the kids. "Everyone get ready to go on." The kids scurried around dressed in their costumes.

"How do I look?" Uncle Jesse asked as he came up to them. He wore a black tuxedo with a red, white, and blue bow tie.

"You look super," said Stephanie.

Joey checked his watch. "You'd better get out there, Jess." Uncle Jesse walked quickly out to the piano in the middle of the stage.

Michelle hurried by dressed as Lady Liberty. "Good luck," Stephanie called to her as she ran out onto the stage. Michelle turned and gave her a thumbs-up. Then she took her place center stage next to the piano. With a smile on her face, she raised her torch high.

Uncle Jesse began to play. The stage curtains parted and the audience cheered.

When the song ended, Joey nudged Aaron. He was dressed in his George Washington costume, with a long blue coat and white wig. "You're on," Joey whispered, giving Aaron a gentle shove.

"Greetings, fellow Americans," said Aaron, walking out onto the stage. "I am the father of our country," he continued. "My name is Aaron Bailey."

"You're George Washington!" Joey whispered to Aaron.

"Oh, yeah," said Aaron. "My name is George Washington." He gestured toward the side of the stage. "And here comes my wife, Bertha."

"Martha!" Joey whispered.

"Martha," Aaron corrected himself.

Stephanie looked at Denise, who waited in the wings dressed in a puffy white wig and a frilly dress with a wide hoopskirt. She didn't seem to realize she was supposed to go onstage. "Denise, you're on," Joey whispered, giving her a little push.

Denise began to walk onstage, but a curl of

her wig had gotten snagged on Joey's metal watchband. As she moved onstage, the wig flew off her head and dangled from Joey's wrist. Denise was already onstage when she realized she didn't have her hair. Quickly Joey tossed the wig out to her.

The audience roared with laughter.

Stephanie took the laughter as a good sign. At least it meant the crowd wasn't bored. They were enjoying themselves. "I think it's going pretty well," she whispered to Joey.

Obviously Joey didn't agree. He just looked toward the ceiling and shook his head in despair.

"Don't worry," Stephanie told him. "I've seen second-grade plays where ten things went wrong in the first five minutes."

"From that point of view, I guess we're doing all right," Joey agreed.

"Sure we are," said Stephanie.

By the third and final act, things were going smoothly. There had been only a couple of mistakes along the way. Stephanie could see that Michelle was getting tired of holding up her torch for such a long time. By the third act she was leaning to one side and holding it with two hands. Still, she was hanging in there, and the show was almost over. Stephanie was proud of her little sister. In the last few days Michelle had really proven she could be a team player. She'd been totally cooperative about the play.

Onstage they were getting ready for the final scene—the big "Yankee Doodle" number. "Good-bye, Paul Revere!" Aaron called to a boy named Michael, who was riding around the stage on a broomstick horse.

"Thanks for the warning," Denise added as she waved to the boy. "Thank goodness he warned us that the British will soon attack."

Hoping all the kids would remember the dance steps, Stephanie crossed her fingers. But with Derek at the center of things, it couldn't go too badly. Derek was so terrific that all eyes would be on him. No one would notice if a few kids were out of step.

Stephanie watched as Michelle stepped forward and said, "Look! Here comes that Yankee Doodle boy!"

They'd added that line to the play just the

day before. Uncle Jesse had decided they needed a line to prepare the audience for the big scene. He'd given the line to Michelle as a way of thanking her for being such a good sport about the play.

Stephanie looked around for Derek. He was supposed to walk onstage right after Michelle said her line. But Stephanie didn't see Derek anywhere.

"I said, Look, here comes that Yankee Doodle boy!" Michelle repeated loudly.

There was still no sign of Derek.

"Where is he?" Stephanie whispered to Joey.

Joey looked all around. "I don't know."

"Excuse me," said Michelle. She handed her torch to a kid who was dressed as Abraham Lincoln.

Michelle walked backstage. "Where is Derek?" she asked Stephanie and Joey.

"Yeah, where is he?" demanded Uncle Jesse, who had rushed away from the piano.

"We don't know," said Joey helplessly.

"Well, we'd better find him," said Uncle Jesse. "And fast!"

NINE

Everyone spread out in all directions, looking for Derek. "He couldn't have gone far," Joey said to Michelle. "He was just here a second ago."

Stephanie quickly found him. He was trying to sneak out the backstage door. When she put her hand on his shoulder, the boy stood absolutely still, not moving a muscle. "Here he is!" she called to the others.

Uncle Jesse, Joey, and Michelle came hurrying over. "Come on, Derek," said Uncle Jesse. "You're on. This is the big finish."

Slowly Derek turned. His eyes were wide with fright. All he could seem to do was shake his head slightly. Stephanie noticed that his hands were trembling.

This was the worst thing that could possibly happen! Without the final act, the show was a dud. "He's frozen!" she said frantically. "The show's over! It's a total choke job."

"Steph," Joey said calmly, "you're not helping matters."

"Sorry," said Stephanie, trying to calm down.

"Derek, come on," said Joey. "You're going to be great."

"No," Derek replied in a very small voice. "I can't do this."

"Let me talk to him," said Michelle, squeezing between Uncle Jesse and Joey. "Derek, do you know how long I've been holding up my arms? You can't let us down now. I didn't let my arms go numb for nothing."

"Michelle, I'm too scared to go out there," Derek said. "You should be Yankee Doodle.

You're really good."

Stephanie expected Michelle to jump at the chance. But she didn't. "Yes, that's true," Michelle said. "But you're great, Derek."

"Right now, I'm sick," Derek insisted.

Stephanie had no trouble believing that. Derek's face was pale, and the trembling in his hands seemed to be traveling up his arms. But even though he was shaking like someone who was cold, tiny beads of sweat had formed on his forehead. His bangs were damp and clumped together.

"We're all on the same team, Derek," Michelle urged him. "We need you."

"You do?" Derek asked.

"Totally," said Michelle. "Now go out there and be the best Yankee Doodle you can be!"

The terrified look slowly left Derek's face. The color began coming back to his cheeks. "Okay," he said. "Here I go."

But a half minute later, he was still standing there.

"You're not moving," Michelle pointed out.

"Give me a push," Derek requested.

Michelle got behind Derek and began pushing. Soon she'd pushed him all the way back to the stage. "Good job, Michelle," said Joey.

"I'm proud of you, peanut," said Uncle Jesse. Then he ran back onto the stage. "Thanks for waiting, everybody," he told the audience. "We're back."

"You'll be great," Michelle told Derek, patting his shoulder. Then she went onstage.

"Now, as I was saying," she spoke to the audience. "Look! Here comes that Yankee Doodle boy!"

With that, Derek sprang out onto the stage.

Stephanie sighed with relief as he began to belt out the song. "I'm a Yankee Doodle dandy, a Yankee Doodle do or die!" He was his old self again.

Michelle smiled and held up her torch proudly. Derek had never been better. She was proud of him, and she was proud of herself. She'd proved she could be a team player.

Derek sang a few more verses, then suddenly he swung his arm out toward Michelle. "Let's go, Miss Liberty!" he cried as he tap-danced in place.

Michelle didn't miss a beat. She took his

hand, and they sang the last chorus together. "Yankee Doodle came to town, riding on a pony! I am that Yankee Doodle boy!"

A line of kids marched out behind them. The leader was Aaron, carrying a big American flag. The audience jumped up and began clapping and cheering.

Michelle smiled so hard her cheeks hurt. It wasn't every team player who also got to be a star, even for just a few minutes.

When the play ended, the whole family went out for ice cream to celebrate. They pushed together two tables and ordered the gooiest sundaes on the menu. "Well," said Danny after they'd ordered. "Considering that was the third time I've seen the play, I'd say this production was certainly a unique version."

"Of course it was," said Uncle Jesse with a smile. "It was directed by two unique and gifted directors."

"And a unique and gifted choreographer," Joey added.

"Plus it had the unique new part of Lady Liberty," said Stephanie. "That added a lot."

"Plus, the super two-Yankee-Doodle finish," said D.J.

"I bet they'll never have one Yankee Doodle again," Becky said. "You've set a new standard for double-Yankee-Doodle excellence."

Michelle smiled happily. "I was good, wasn't I?"

"The best," said Danny. "You know, I've learned something these last few weeks."

"What?" Stephanie asked with a mischievous grin. "To check earlobes the minute your daughter starts to resemble Princess Leah?"

"Well, yes," said Danny. "But that wasn't what I was about to say. What I've learned is that each of my daughters is special and *unique*, in her own way. The three of you are alike in some ways, but different in others. From now on I'm going to respect those differences."

"Does that mean we don't have to wear any more hand-me-down clothes?" Michelle asked.

"Ah . . . no, it doesn't mean that," said Danny.

"Well, can we at least get rid of the matching pajama sets?" asked Stephanie.

"Absolutely," Danny agreed.

"And no more three-of-a-kind pocketbook presents each September at the start of school?" D.J. asked hopefully.

Danny frowned. "I thought you liked those."

"I *do* like getting a new pocketbook," said D.J. "But could we each have a different pocketbook?

"You got it," Danny agreed.

"All right!" Stephanie, Michelle, and D.J. cried all together. Just then, the sundaes arrived. Everyone dove in.

"You know what's funny?" said Stephanie. "Michelle wanted to be like D.J. and me. But I wanted to be different from D.J."

"But I just want to be me now," Michelle spoke up.

"Good," said Danny. "Being you is exactly who I want you to be."

As Michelle ate, she noticed that Stephanie was looking at her and smiling. "I'm proud of you, Michelle," she said quietly.

"I'm proud of you too, Oh Earringless

One," Michelle replied softly.

Under the table, they shook hands. It was great to be sisters—the same and yet different in so many wonderful ways.